Johanna M Sanders

Poems and Ballads

Johanna M Sanders

Poems and Ballads

ISBN/EAN: 9783337376710

Printed in Europe, USA, Canada, Australia, Japan

Cover: Foto ©Andreas Hilbeck / pixelio.de

More available books at **www.hansebooks.com**

POEMS AND BALLADS

BY

JOHANNA M. SANDERS

SAN FRANCISCO
PRINTED PRIVATELY FOR THE AUTHOR
BRUNT & COMPANY
1890

Of One Hundred Copies Printed

This is No.

TO MY GRANDSON
ALFRED ALLISON WHEELER
THESE POEMS ARE AFFECTIONATELY
DEDICATED

Contents

POEMS AND BALLADS

MY SONG

WHAT though my lips be mute
　　Or faintly sighing,
Like some unfingered lute
　　Neglected lying,
Amid whose silver chords sweet music only
　　　　slumbers
Until the minstrel's touch shall wake its hidden
　　　　numbers :—
　　Within my bosom sealed,
　　　Oft wildly ringing,—
　　The music unrevealed,—
　　　My heart is singing.

　　Like haunting sounds that dwell
　　　With soft emotion
　　In pearly cavern'd shell,
　　　Borne from the ocean,
Throbbing in echoed pulse to distant billows'
　　　　swelling,
Their solemn melodies in mystic whispers
　　　　telling :—
　　A mem'ry of the skies,
　　　In music clinging,
　　Within my fond heart lies,
　　　Forever singing.

And though my lips be mute
Or faintly sighing,
Bearing no outward fruit
Of that inlying,
And though no touch of fire, in words of kindling
glory,
With bardic gift translate my spirit's silent
story :—
Its own true song of life
In secret winging,
My heart, unmoved by strife,
Is ever singing.

MAY DAY .

I

WAKE, comrades! Lightly spring
From slumber's drowsy thrall!
Cheerful hearts and voices bring,
Responsive to our call.
Come, come, come merrily, comrades all !
With a joyous lay
To greet the day,
And lead forth our bonny Queen of May.
Crown her with roses, glowing buds
Impearled with dew;
And scarf her bosom pure with braids
Of violets blue;
The sceptre, token of her power,
A slender wand
Of fragrant lilies, spotless white,
Place in her hand,
As chosen queen of our happy band.

II

Then haste to the upland lawn,
Gemmed with the breath of night,
While the silver-footed dawn
Comes dancing o'er the height,
And Nature smiles in answering delight.

With lips as gay,
Shout, shout away,
All hail to our bonny Queen of May!
On! lead her to the throne of state—
The rustic chair
Of twisted branches quaintly made,
That lichens bear;
Her dainty foot-stool mosses be,—
The carpet green
Where moonlit elves and flitting fays
Erst danced unseen,
In antic mirth with their own fair queen.

III

Let our heartfelt music swell
In chorus loud and deep,
Wafted to the secret cell
Where sportive echoes sleep;
Till cheerily every woody steep
In mocking play
Sweet homage pay,
And ring to our bonny Queen of May.
Her canopy the spreading shade
Of stately oak,
Whose hoary stem has braved the storm
And thunder-stroke,
Now garlanded, like smiling age,
With honied vines,—
The woodbine's wealth and blushing grace
Of eglantines,
Blazoned in trembling gold with furtive shines.

IV

Choicest posies hither bring
   From rifled field or nook,
Moist from green-enameled spring
   And lily-margined brook,
Or formal plats that garden walls o'erlook.
     To the May-pole gay,
     Away, away!
Then bear off our bonny Queen of May!
   With leafy banners shedding sweets
     From purple plumes
   Of lilac branch, and rosy crests
     Of chestnut blooms.
   Emblems of innocence and joy
     Her path bestrew!
   Oh, may her life's light footsteps press
     On flowers too,
That wear serenest tints of pleasure's hue!

V

Nimbly, nimbly on the green,
   Dance now and gaily sing;
Hands entwining each between,
   Quickly form the fairy ring;
And drooping wreaths like fragrant censers swing.
     Dance, dance, dance away!
     No foot may stay.
Dance about our bonny Queen of May!
   With airy laughter, jokes and wiles
     From boys and girls,
   And flaunting ribbons letting fall

Long sunny curls,
　We trip the giddy circle round
　　With hearts of glee,
　Nor pause the frolic step, till by
　　Our queen set free,
To cast our glowing tributes at her knee.

VI

Like gazelles whose bounding feet
　O'er perfumed prairies go,
Seeking some beloved retreat
　In fertile valleys low,
Where spring breathes soft and waters flow,
　　To wander and play
　　The livelong day,
We run with our bonny Queen of May:
　Some to the fountain's bubbling brink
　　With thirsty lip;
　Some to the shady stream, their lines
　　To slyly dip;
　To the pied meads and clover fields
　　Of emerald sheen,
　To lure the bees and butterflies
　　The blooms between,
Or oracles from sibyl daisies glean.

VII

Gather, gather, rovers all,
　With lagging step and slow!
To rest in groves where shadows fall
　That noon-gleams never know,—
To the May-feast gather at the call!

Who'd stop to play,—
When called away
To feast with our bonny Queen of May?
Then ere we part, we'll saunter through
Some sylvan glade,
Or musky woodland's arching aisles
Of mottled shade ;
List to wild minstrelsy afloat
On the still air ;
Peer into ferny brakes and thorns
For nestlings there ;
Or watch the squirrel sport, or start the hare.

VIII

Homeward, birds ! On weary wing,
One lingering pause devote,
To join in grateful caroling,
With latest, sweetest note,
That haply may to heaven's portal float ;
For in twilight grey,
Fast fades away
The reign of our bonny Queen of May.
' Spread o'er her couch, O balmy Sleep,
Thy charméd veil !
Let gentle Shapes kind vigil keep,
Till stars grow pale ! '
Lo ! now the crescent moon betrays
Its tender light ;
And rippling on the dewy air,
' Good night ! Good night ! '
Proclaims our May-day revels ended quite.

On the Rhine

SWIFTLY flows the dark blue Rhine,
  Like a Sibyl, half divine,
Murmuring, as it glides along,
Many a weird and wondrous song,
Red with strife and strong with pride,
And mellowed by time, like the fiery wine
Of sunny vineyards by its side :—
Songs of love, the olden story ;
Songs of tournay, war, and glory ;
Songs of age and songs of youth ;
Of holy strivings after truth,
And darkest deeds of hate or ruth.

O bright river, storied river,
Siren-tongued, immortal Rhine,
What entrancing lays are thine !
What rugged rhymes and dreamy chimes
Of those heroic, struggling times,
To listening ears dost thou deliver !

Once more upon thy shining breast,
In fancy's magic colors drest,

Oh, let the mirrored outline rest
Of wooded hills and castled steep,
Embattled towers and frowning keep ;
Let blazoned banners proudly float
O'er bold escarp and guarded moat ;
Bid Time restore dismantled halls,
The ivied arch, the crumbled walls ;
And 'mid thy vines and fruity bowers,
And waving fields and crowding flowers,
Bring back the pageant, martial host,
The battle cry and lordly boast,
The steel-clad warrior stout and brave,
The glancing spear and flashing glaive.
The war-steed decked with housings bright.
And noble bearing of the knight,
In gallant deeds of high emprise
To win the smile of ladies' eyes.

Sing on, sing on, thou stately stream !
The artist's love, the poet's dream !
Sing of fair maids and bandits dun.
Of spectres grim and cloistered nun,
Of giant heroes, empires won,
And precious blood on every hand
Shed for the love of Fatherland !
Awake earth's echoes far and wide
With lofty hymns, first sung beside
The cradle of an Infant Truth
That strangled serpents in its youth,
And whose maturing strength has brought
Freedom to man's aspiring thought !

Sing on ! and let me catch the sigh
Of dying years that round thee lie,
The spirit and the old emotion
Of melodies that with thee fly
To mingle with Oblivion's ocean.

THE LOST PLEIAD

MEROPÈ, child of light, why dost thou haste
  From realms where thou hast dwelt
    serenely chaste?
  Why, ah why yearn
To view life's turbulent sad sights,
And share, with human passion, blights
  That chill or burn?

Seeking a mortal spouse in earth's dark maze,
Doth not some vision on thy steadfast gaze
    Forboding wake?
  And with dim prophecy of pain—
  From love unsatisfied or slain—
    Thy purpose shake?

Thy star grows pale, where, in a golden throng,
Thy sister Pleiads wake celestial song;
    For nevermore,
  Amid that shimmering, star-linked band,
  Shalt thou, Earth-bound Meropè, stand
    As heretofore.

The Singer

A LADY sat within her bower
      Once on a day,—
Lily-fair, in the golden hour
      Of youth's sweet May ;
But brighter than day's golden shower,
And sweeter than spring's opening flower,
Dwelt in her breast a latent power,—
      Fatal alway !
An altar and a tomb the dower
      Of Passion's sway.

II

From the pure fountains of her heart,
      So deep and strong,
Came gushing, her ripe lips apart,
      The tide of song :
Hymning of joy and life and art,
As thoughts to forms of beauty start,
Or playful fancies glance and dart,—
      Like doves that throng
On white wings fluttering to depart
      And flight prolong.

III

Each passing footstep lingered there,
  So sweetly fell
That lofty music, with a rare
  Melodious spell:
Easing the burdened mind of care,
Soothing the anguish of despair,
Teaching the suffering soul to bear
  Or grief dispel :—
So prodigal its strength to share,
  Its joy to tell.

IV

Till faltering ceased those anthems clear ;
  As ebbing streams
Pause, stilled, when tidal pulses near.
  (O rosy dreams !
In whose illusive atmosphere
So radiantly hopes appear,
That vanish with a sigh, a tear,
  In misty gleams !)
Love's presence wakes a tender fear
  That rapture seems.

V

With outstretched arms and bosom bare
  To the pure light,
She softly wooes that phantom fair
  Of new delight,—
For heart of heart craves equal share ;

When lo, a shadow falling there,
She only clasps the empty air;
  And lost to sight,
The vision fades on her despair,—
  Love's early blight!

VI

But the pent song that erst was still—
  (Alas, that grief
Had power its sunny flow to chill
  In unbelief!)—
Burst through the bonds of baffled will
With richer melody to thrill,
And sweeter, deeper sense instill.
  (Just so the leaf
Is shed, when nectared juices fill
  Their fruity sheath.)

VII

Yet mingling tones of sadness came,
  Unheard before:
The fainting cry of want and pain
  Without the door,
The craving else than empty fame,
The shrinking from a touch of blame,
The thirst of a consuming flame,—
  Ah, how deplore
Those shuddering discords that proclaim
  The reft heart's lore!

VIII

Till with soft show of courtesy
    And wooing bland,—
(So weds the secret, treacherous sea
    The smiling land)—
A stately form on bended knee
Proffers the chalice that should be
A charméd draught, her song to free
    From sorrow's brand.
(The luring hand of Destiny
    Who may withstand?)

IX

But oh, her bowed lips only greet
    A bitter taste!
And heart-stung by her love's defeat,—
    Recking no waste
That makes a sacrifice complete,—
Into that cup, woe's last retreat,
She throws her life! (Love's gains are fleet!)
    Pouring, thus graced,
The rich libation at his feet
    With fatal haste.

X

The light has faded from the west;
    Come the dark hour;
Death sits a grim and silent guest
    Within the bower.
Her white hands folded on her breast,

Like snow-wreaths from an Alpine crest,
The lovely minstrel lies at rest,—
    A broken flower !
At peace for aye the heart oppressed
    By passion's power.

XI

But that high song's immortal sound
    Still echoes, heard
Above the din of life's dull round,
    And souls are stirred :
The brow of thought with rapture crowned,
And hearts from chains of earth unbound,
When with electric touch profound
    Some burning word
Sheds with its light a joy new-found
    On hope deferred!

THE SECRET CAIRN

ABOVE the grave of perished joys
    And daring hopes untimely slain,
There rises, stone by stone, a Cairn,
    Secreted in the heart's domain ;
Where pilgrim thoughts, through weary years,
Oft pause with unavailing tears.

The flaunting trains of worldly pride
    Pass by afar and know it not ;
No warring passions linger there
    To desecrate the hallowed spot
Where souls bereaved, with mournful song,
Unceasing requiems prolong.

Love only waits and vigil keeps,
    Through the long night of grief's dark hours;
Till from oblivion's gathering mould
    Spring memory's amaranthine flowers,
And faith's pure dawn, with promise bright,
Touches the Secret Cairn with light.

THE TRUANT LORD

HE cries to his horse, as with loosened rein
    He spurs and bounds o'er the barren
      plain,—
"On, Selim, on ! high-hearted steed,
That never yet failed me at my need !
Miles upon miles before us lie,
Now prove your mettle and onward fly."

The rider bethinks him of his home,—
In an evil hour he had willed to roam,—
Of its sparkling founts, its vine-hung bowers,
Its alleys green, its fruits and flowers;
Of his fair young wife, of a voice unheard,
Of the charm and joy of a loving word.

But none of these to his restless heart
Could the balm of sweet content impart.
He longed for action and power and state,
To vie with men and to war with fate ;
And so it befell on a weary day,
He mounted his Arab and rode away.

Then days and months and years were told,
And the fervor of early love grew cold ;
Till in a vision of import dire,

An angel kindled remorseful fire ;
And his heart cried out with craving pain
For love and the sweets of home again.

Though brave the steed and swift his flight,
His flanks with red and his breast with white
Are with blood and foam bedabbled o'er,
Ere breathless he stops at his master's door.
No loving smile, no welcoming word,
By the truant Lord is seen or heard.

On a bed of slime, unmoved and dim,
The water sleeps at the fountain's rim ;
Where beauty of art with nature vied,
The newt and the slug in silence glide ;
Ungarnered fruits decay and drop ;
Thistles and weeds are summer's crop.

The spider has woven her silken lace
To drape the portal's dingy face ;
Over ruined garden and empty hall,
Behold ! there hangs a funereal pall
For hope departed and love betrayed
And a broken heart in the tomb low-laid.

TINTERN ABBEY

THERE stands in ruin Tintern's hallowed
    fane,
Where silence, awe and desolation reign !

Through roofless walls, here ages yet entire,
No longer heavenward points the lofty spire ;
Its deep foundations, too, arched o'er in vain,
Return with slow decay to earth again.
Some stately columns, time awhile defied,
Still rear their ivied heads with seeming pride ;
Whilst others, fallen from their Gothic state,
With flowers o'ergrown, half hide their humbled
    fate.

Through windows once with pictured story bright,
No more the morning plays with changeful light ;
But clustering vines the casements darkly shade
With graceful fringe of tendrils overlaid ;
And moss and lichens, in each crevice caught,
Quaint traceries of arabesque have wrought.
Tall ferns that in green tangled tresses stream ;
Pale wall-flowers that like golden censers gleam,
Wafting their fragrant incense on the breeze ;
Thistles and grasses in a living frieze,
Together with the ivy's curtained flow,—

A solemn, soft and checkered shadow throw
Along the dew-damp aisle with turf o'erspread,
Where once the pavement holy footsteps led.

Rude pious-sculptured fragments lie around,
And Death's denoting tablets mark his ground;
Whilst tombs to rank and friendship passed away,
Now unremembered, moulder in decay.
The very names that once were known to fame,
Or cherished in fond hearts like sacred flame,
Though graved on marble by the hand of care,
Have vanished like a breath upon the air.

Yon stairway, which, by fearful footing traced,
Still hangs almost in air through years of waste,
Once coursed secure the turret's circled height,
Where lonely monk, in prayer th' enduring night,
With contrite heart essayed and bitter tears
To lull remorse or soothe fanatic fears.
Or there perhaps some deep, ambitious mind,
Mysterious vigils kept, in thought sublimed;
Aimed by forbidden art and magic spell
The star-stampt characters of night to tell;
But secrets dire perused of hidden fate
Still left the lonely heart more desolate.

No tinkling bell, nor organ's swelling sound,
Nor chanting voice breaks silence oft profound.
The screech-owl's vesper cry alone is heard,
Or matin music of some flitting bird.
No joy-bells thrill the golden morning air
With bridal summons for the young and fair;

No pealing chimes of Merrie Christmas tell,
Nor solemn tolling of the passing knell ;
But summer breezes mournful music wake,
And wintry winds more awful dirges make,
When flooding rains like tears unnumbered fall,
Or drifting snow-wreaths spread a ghastly pall.

And yet within this desecrated fane,
Like lingering perfume, hallowed things remain :
The dew of contrite tears ; the breath of prayer
That once exhaled upon its sacred air ;
The dust of holy men and weary life,
That here laid down their burdens, ceased their
　　　strife,
And 'neath the shelter of a common sod
Found peace within the bosom of their God.

On a Piece of Washington's Coffin

A RELIC—dumb, yet oh ! how eloquent—
This fragment of the lowly, narrow bed
Of him for whom a nation's tears were shed !
Who, in the hour of need, his genius lent
To heal his country's wounds,—war's fury spent ;
And having patriot hosts to conquest led,
In peace, unsullied by ambition, spread
Fresh lustre on Free People's Government.

Less frail this remnant of the forest tree
Than mortal shell now crumbled into dust ;
But noble deeds and truth and honor live
Immortal ; and till time shall cease to be,
The name of Washington to all men must
Be hallowed and the hope of freedom give.

THE STARS AND STRIPES

A BALLAD OF THE FIRST VICTIM OF THE

CIVIL WAR

THE blow that lowered Sumter's flag
    Awoke a slumbering fire
That gathered lightnings on its path
    To weld a people's ire.
That blow, aimed at a Nation's life,
    Struck every loyal heart,
And taught the scheming partisan
    The patriot's nobler part;

Respect for just, enlightened rule,
    Obedience to Law,—
Voice of his country's majesty
    That Anarchy shall awe ;
To keep the Starry Flag aloft,
    Unsullied and unshorn,
A beacon-hope on Freedom's height
    For ages yet unborn;

And more than life to prize that bond
    Whose wise control unites
The strength of numbers with the pride
    Of individual rights;

Which knows not East, West, North nor South,
    Save one united Whole :
One name, one past, one destiny,
    One body and one soul.

A brooding horror filled the pause,
    Dread herald of the storm,
Ere the avenging hand was raised
    Or severed thought could form ;
Till burst the war-cloud's pent up wrath,
    And borne from hill to shore,
A Nation's mortal cry went forth :—
    "Onward! through Baltimore !"

" Columbia calls her loyal sons
    To ward off Treason's guile ;
To quell the parricidal rage
    That would her soil defile ;
To guard her stately Capitol
    From the invading tread
Of rebel children, who would pour
    Dishonor on her head !"

Then from the workshop and the field,
    The anvil and the loom,
The press, the studio, the school,
    The mart and counting-room,
Came heart to heart, like brethren true
    Their birthright to defend,
The heirs of freedom bought with blood,
    Their own free blood to spend.

Foremost in answer to that call,
    Among the loyal ones
With noble indignation fired,
    Came stern New England's sons.
They came in faith but to defend
    The Nation's Temple-door ;
No order yet to draw the sword,
    But "On ! through Baltimore ! "

Too honest all to apprehend
    Rebellion's brutal power,
Mob-force, that met them shamelessly
    In that unguarded hour ;
Assailed with missiles rude and vile,
    And shot like beasts of prey :—
Such welcome Baltimore bestowed
    On that fair April day.

O city of historic pride,
    Wipe off that bloody stain !
Untarnished raise the civic shield
    With loyalty again !
Bright gem that sparkles on the brow
    Of haughty Maryland,
For Freedom and for Union shine
    Among the starry band !

Where thickest fall the dastard blows,
    First fruit of Treason's hate,
A wounded youth unnoticed lies :
    Achieved a hero's fate !

A solemn calm to pain succeeds,
    He watches from afar
The flag he no more may defend,
    So long his guiding star.

When lo ! as though the parting soul
    Would bear to heaven's expanse
Some shadow of its Past, recalled
    In one supernal glance,—
Sweet visions minister delight,
    While death holds revel there :
The pageant of his guiltless life
    Seems painted on the air.

New Hampshire's wooded heights ! O joy—
    The sweets of home once more !
The swallows building in the eaves
    Above the cottage door ;
The rustic garden where he watched
    The resurrected seed,—
That oracle of Nature's love
    Which he who runs may read ;

The ancient musket on the wall,
    Revered with childish awe,
His gallant grandsire once had borne
    At glorious Chippewa ;
The old man's stirring tales of war
    Beside the winter hearth,
Of victories and moral throes
    That gave a nation birth;

His boyish aspirations for
  Some greatness undefined,
His trivial faults, privations, joys,
  Are strangely brought to mind :
How, when the daily task was done,
  In some secluded nook
His country's history he conned
  From the long-treasured book ;

How to the drum and fife's glad sound
  His heart would wildly beat,
As proudly near the village corps
  He trod the grass-grown street ;
How sprang the hot, unconscious tears
  To eyes unused to weep,
When o'er those native skies he saw
  The Flag of Freedom sweep ;

And how, when war's imperious call
  Disturbed this dreamy life,
He woke to manhood, joined the ranks,
  And parted for the strife.
And then his little brother's wish,
  Half sorrow and half pride,—
"O sister, would I were a man,
  To fight by Jamie's side !"

That sister's artless vanity
  To see his martial grace ;
The tearless pallor, like a veil,
  Spread o'er his mother's face ;

Her last fond look, her parting words—
"My son, be true and brave!"—
When to the country's treasury
Her Widow's Mite she gave.

But memory fades with ebbing life,
And instinct guides the way
To drag his failing limbs beyond
The tumult of the fray.
A humble shop is near, he gains
At last a shelter there,
Where pity wakes and gentle hands
Bestow a Christian care.

But one stands by with sullen brow
And cold, embittered heart,
Who calls himself a "Southerner,"
And takes a traitor's part;
Who falsely claims secession's right
The Union to destroy,
And looks with sectional disdain
Upon the "Yankee" boy.

To him unknown the generous glow
That fired that patriot breast,
Its simple faith—Obedience
To loyalty's behest;
A selfish policy he knew,
The partisan's poor lore;
And rudely questioned and rebuked—
This man of Baltimore.

"Unlucky boy ! what brought you here
　　To face the brunt of war ?
The workshop or the school, methinks,
　　Were more befitting far ;
Or mother's chiding hand to curb
　　A vanity so mad :—
Say, was it for the ' hireling's pay ? '
　　What brought you here, my lad ?"

The youthful hero, rallying
　　His fast departing breath,
Uplifts a pallid brow where hang
　　The icy beads of death ;
The radiance of a heavenly smile
　　Played o'er his ghastly cheek,
As thrice his faltering lips essayed
　　The proud reply to speak.

Forth from his wide and filmy eye
　　There flashed a sudden fire ;
One last great throb his true heart gave,
　　As woke the old desire.
Then, as he sank—to rise no more—
　　Upon his gory bed,
In thrilling, sweet, exultant tone,
　　" *The Stars and Stripes !*" he said.

A Centennial Ode

JULY 4, 1876

I

COLUMBIA ! like some goddess newly shrined
  In Time's emblazoned hall, thou'st made
    thy name
A talisman of hope for faith to bind
  Above the wounds of nations and their shame !
  Thy banner, Freedom's glorious oriflame,
Hath borne to many a land o'er ocean's bound
  A blessing with the triumph of thy fame,
And wakened in man's heart a joy profound,
Where'er thy watchword, " Liberty," was heard
    to sound.

II

Quick with regenerate force, thou wert a Bud
  To be engrafted on the virgin years ;
A new Evangel, written with the blood
  Of trodden peoples and their children's tears ;
  A Sign portentous waking tyrants' fears ;
A Haven made for Pilgrim feet that fled
  The cruel barriers Superstition rears :—
Star of the West, thy kindling radiance led
To Freedom's cradled hope, and holy influence
    shed !

III

The tangled forest, the unpeopled wild—
   Or peopled only with a savage race—
Were braved and conquered, nature's frowns
     beguiled,
   Until the desert bloomed with every grace.
   Danger and want to free, full life gave place ;
And faith's endurance, life's heroic toils,
   Gave strength to growth which now moves on
     apace,
Laden with wisdom's wealth and nature's spoils,
From whose enlightened bulwarks ignorance
   recoils.

IV

Let Pride and pompous Ceremonial pause
   Ere they decry the rudeness of thy youth,
Or curl the haughty lip of scorn, because
   Thy monuments historic are, forsooth,
   Not yet embellished by Time's gnawing tooth ;
For thou hast reared a pharos on thy shore,
   The Light of Freedom, nature's sacred truth,
Where panting slaves and exiles sad and sore
Shall feel oppression's goad and burdens never-
   more !

V

Thy temple doors have opened to the world
   A sanctuary for enfranchised Mind ;
Beneath thy starry flag, in peace unfurled,
   Trophies of industry and art are twined ;
   Just laws and equal rights the fasces bind ;

There in one universal brotherhood
   All nationalities a home may find,
The fruits of liberty—their daily food—
May gather and enjoy, if rightly understood.

VI

The treasures of primeval days are stored
   In earth's kind breast throughout thy vast
      domains ;
From Plenty's horn a lavish sweetness poured
   On fruitful valleys and wide grassy plains ;
   While o'er blue lakes and winding river veins
A spirit of ethereal beauty bends,
   O'er the steep cataract's abysses reigns,
On snow-clad mounts and giant groves descends,
And grandeur's grace to Nature's wilder aspects
      lends.

VII

And many a name of hero and of sage,
   Serene in peace, in war still undismayed,
Illuminates thy brief historic page.
   The name of Washington, with pride displayed
   On thy emblazoned shield, a shrine hath made
In every land where an aspiring soul
   Its sacrifice on freedom's altar laid.
Long may that hallowed name, while cycles roll,
Be cherished and thy sons' ambitious aims
      control!

VIII

The fire of war's dissension quenched—a flame
   By error kindled and by passion fed—

Aggressive hands, once raised with deadly aim,
　In friendship clasp ; grief's mutual tears are
　　　shed—
All wrongs forgotten of the buried dead—
O'er many a grave of brother once a foe :
　Embittered hearts that once in discord bled,
Now gladly throb with patriot pride, and know
The blessings union, peace and liberty bestow.

IX

Thy grateful sons, Columbia, greet thee now
　First hallowed by a century of years !
Years whose immortal fruits shall yet endow
　Humanity with youthful strength that cheers,
　And moral beauty, as new light appears.
And though the mazy paths of truth elude
　Man's groping mind awhile, though error rears
Its hydra-head in vile solicitude,—
Years of unfettered thought may lead to Perfect
　Good.

X

A century of chartered freedom thine-—
　The first imperial stamp by ages prest;
Victorious bays and peaceful olives twine
　Thy starry diadem's refulgent crest.
　Thy pedestal a New World, thou dost rest
With firm feet on a mighty continent,
　A boundless ocean laving either breast,
Thine eyes upon a glorious future bent ;
Humanity's Ideal ! Freedom's Embodiment !

Dalilah

'T IS done ! the deed of treachery and guile
    That robs the mighty warrior of his
        strength !
His shorn locks lie in all their vaunted length
Beneath thy feet, the spoil of many a wile ;
And gold thy cruel fair hands doth defile,
    Thou type of perjured woman's evil ways,
    Who while caressing secretly betrays,
And stabs at life and honor with a smile !

Upon thy brow, now passionless and cold,
    As though remorse stirred in thy stony heart,
The moral of thy guilty tale is told
In conscious shame :—a germ of heavenly mould,
    Left, ere thy better angel did depart,
    To bloom in pity there, immortalized by Art.

Florence Nightingale

A NGEL of help, by holy fires annealed,
    Whose charméd name links with Italia's
        flower
The wakeful minstrel of the rosy bower,
How oft thy voice like music's balm hath healed
Despair and anguish death alone had sealed,
    When e'en thy shadow's sympathetic power,
    Through thy sweet mercies, soothed the dying
        hour
Of heroes, and their fainting hearts were steeled.

Then like the Swan-White Maiden's fairy spell,
    The " precious gems "—of thought by truth
        made bold,
    The " golden rings "—of love's encircling fold,
In countless blessings from thy presence fell ;
    And in the vital warmth thy good deeds shed,
    Sprang roses whereso'er thy footsteps led.

THE BRIDE

H ER bridal robes all pearly white,
   Of silvery, silken gleams,
Seem luminous as fleecy clouds
   That veil the moon's chaste beams ;
And filmy laces fall like foam
   That follows in her wake,
As to the sacred shrine she glides,
   Love's plight to give and take.

With eyes like violets bathed in dew,
   Downcast in maiden shame,
And fluttering heart impressed with awe
   And fears without a name ;
While orange-blooms, the virgin crown,
   Their fragrant breath exhale
Above a fair unsullied brow
   And cheeks as lilies pale.

As on some far rock-columned shore
   Resounding billows swell,
And breaking die, soft as the sigh
   Within an ocean shell,—
The organ's deep melodious tides
   In wavy raptures rise,

And choral voices thrill and melt
  Like sounds from Paradise.

With heart to heart, for bliss or bale,
  The youthful spouses stand ;
The golden circlet of the wife
  Gleams on the bride's fair hand ;
Her pledge of love, life's freight of hope,
  In trust supreme is given :—
Oh, may that vow be blest on earth
  And registered in heaven !

THE APPLE WOMAN'S STORY

WILL you buy an apple, madam? Here's a
pippin bright as gold.
Better never ripened,—and many a fine one I
have sold.
Here's red and russet, less beautiful, but just as
sweet and sound.
Thank you, lady. Little Miss will have a treat
now, I'll be bound.

It warms my heart to see her beaming face, so
pure and mild.
'T is a glimpse of heaven,—the darling! Be not
afraid, dear child;
Though I'm like the sere and blasted tree, it was
not always so;
I once was ruddy and straight and strong,—a
long, long time ago.

And I'm so accustomed to it now, I quite forget
the shame
Of my scars and crooked limbs. True, ma'am,
misfortune is no blame;
I've never looked upon a glass since I learnt to
look within,
And face the ugliness found there,—for ah, who
is free from sin?

Yes, I'm growing old, dear lady, shall be sixty-
    nine to-morrow.
I've had sore trials in my time, too, heaps upon
    heaps of sorrow ;
Yet I don't repine, there's nothing now can grieve
    me evermore,
And I'm thankful I have not to beg my bread
    from door to door.

Tell you about it ? Yes, I will. 'T is a dreary
    tale of woe,
That now seems like a troubled dream, for it
    happened long ago.
You can scarce believe, my dear, that I was once
    a pretty girl,
With eyes as bright and blue as yours and as
    many a golden curl.

I was a loved and happy child, though reared on
    plainest food,
And my home the humblest cottage that in our
    village stood.
No lighter step than mine was seen, no merrier
    voice was heard,
In the meadows where I tossed the hay and
    caroled like a bird.

I had many suitors,—and might have married
    better to be sure ;
Yet I was rich in my Harry's love ; fond hearts
    are never poor.

Father and mother—they'd only me—I left for him
    I chose ;
And parting was my heart's first grief, but so
    God's order goes.

Folks said we were a handsome pair. A proud
    and joyous wife,
I little thought my path would lead through
    years of lonely life.
We left the village for the town for the sake of
    Harry's trade :—
A ship-carpenter, my dear, and a good livelihood
    he made.

Snugly and happily we lived, as small comforts
    round us grew.
A blessing rested on us then,—twice a mother's
    joy I knew.
The pretty ways of baby, the prattle of our
    chubby lad,
A tidy hearth and a loving smile, made the home-
    welcome glad.

One evening, keeping holiday, we went to see the
    play,
Leaving our blooming baby Rose with a neighbor
    by the way.
Ann had a nursling of her own ; there seemed
    no reason for regret :
Yet I had misgivings, and my lips with baby's
    tears were wet.

So I wearied of the mirth and glare; and at
    nature's mute demand,
More than once my tingling bosom seemed to feel
    her playful hand.
Silent I sat, and o'er me came a shuddering, name-
    less fear,
As mournful sounds like sobs and cries seemed to
    murmur in my ear.

The curtain fell, we hurried forth. Then, like a
    surging ocean,
The clang of bells, the cry of " Fire!" the engine's
    rushing motion,
Grew louder as we neared our home, lighted by
    lurid flashes,
Alas! to find a blackened ruin, a heap of smoulder-
    ing ashes.

Clasping our boy, my husband parted from me in
    the throng.
I, thinking of baby's peril only, hurried along.
Unmindful of the fiery rain—oh, 't was like the
    day of doom !—
I reached the burning tenement and flew up to
    Annie's room.

Dizzied and blind, I searched and called despair-
    ingly in vain;
Stunned by terror for a moment, then a prey to
    doubt and pain ;
Till a sharp cry, an infant's wail, my groping
    footsteps led :—

From the floor I snatched the darling to my
    breast and would have fled.

But oh, the stairs had vanished! in their place
    great bursts of flame,
Mixed with hissing streams and stifling gusts,
    nearer and nearer came.
Cries of horror from the crowd answered my
    voice, with anguish keen,
When at the window, 'gainst the light, mother
    and babe were seen.

Daring arms were stretched and caught the
    precious little life I bore.
Then from fiery death escaping, I sprang out and
    knew no more.
But oh, I left the hospital a hideous thing, half
    blind and lame ;
And 't was Ann's baby I had saved; mine perished
*   in the flame.*

Yes, lady, Ann was rescued from the attic crazed
    with fright,
Whither she ran to rouse her boys, who else had
    waked no more that night.
Ann said she never could repay me, she a poor
    sailor's wife ;
And would insist she 'd been to blame, good soul,
    and thought so all her life.

Well, health returned, yet every day saw hopes of
    happiness depart ;

For husband never was the same, he took our
    losses so to heart.
Moody or wild, neglecting work, he sought the
    tavern's hateful spell :—
Ah, guess what followed, ma'am, his shame is
    not for my poor tongue to tell.

I struggled on, toiled early and late, more than
    my strength could bear ;
Though Charlie's little gains ere long were
    proudly brought for me to share.
Then happened what I'd long foreseen, after years
    of silent woe,—
But oh, the tears of widowhood came with a
    bitter flow.

Sad and lonely were the days I passed while
    Charlie was at sea.
He was a beautiful, brave boy, and so dutiful to
    me
That I had no heart to thwart his wish to lead
    a sailor's life.
Thank God ! there never came between us a word
    of blame or strife.

He was wondrous clever, too, I still can see his
    sunny smile,
While telling marvelous long yarns, dear boy! our
    evenings to beguile.
I know not how he learnt it all ; his tongue, so
    glib, was never bold,

And so truthful—why, he'd not have told a lie
  for mines of gold.

Well, a hard winter came, when food was dear
  and scarce beside ;
But I sold no apples in those days ; Charlie all
  my wants supplied.
I counted every lengthening day, as a miser
  counts his store,
For with the spring would come my treasure to
  my arms once more.

I remember how I used to sit and watch the little
  star
He once told me guided mariners, wandering on
  seas afar ;
And how my yearning heart would throb, as I
  walked at eve alone,
Looking out upon the ocean, saddened by its
  solemn moan.

And oh, I never, never shall forget when the
  great storm began,
How the wind howled at the shattered pane and
  the rain in torrents ran ;
How I held my fainting breath at the awful
  thunder of the deep,
As all night long I wept and prayed, and never
  thought of sleep.

And what a mortal dread I felt, when, cowering
  at the hearth,

An icy kiss upon my brow left a farewell *not of
    earth*.
A stillness fell ere morning broke ; and when I
    looked upon the street,
The white snow lay in drifted folds like a glisten-
    ing winding-sheet.

Three fearful days the tempest raged, before 't was
    truly known,
That, while saving other lives, my boy had
    bravely lost his own;
And that almost in sight of home his ship had
    gone ashore,
Freighted with precious souls, whose little dream
    of life was o'er.

Small comfort to me was it then to hear his
    frozen corse was found,
And with others decently interred in consecrated
    ground.
But now I'm glad to know he sleeps beneath the
    heaven's blue pall,
With a sunny sod upon his breast where summer
    roses fall.

You weep,—ay, so did I those days, until my
    heart was dry.
But now I'm waiting patiently to join them all
    on high.
I've earned a pittance, just enough a pauper's end
    to save ;

And have a spotless suit laid by to clothe me for
    the grave.

I cannot see through it all ! yet I *feel* that God is
    good,
That His sacred promises are kept, though not
    always understood.
No kindred branch is left me, but He has lent a
    little flower
To cheer my wintry age and dew with tears its
    last dark hour.

'Tis Nellie, madam, Ann's poor grandchild, now
    orphaned and alone.
I love the dear good girl, and oftentimes forget
    she 's not my own.
On holidays and the brief hours that labor leaves
    to spare,
She never fails to come and soothe me with many
    a tender care.

Together then we gossip and the pleasant time
    flies fast,
While she prophecies the future and I preach
    about the past.
And that is all my story, dear. Yes, when it's
    not too cold,
You 'll find me hereabouts,—not long, though,
    for I'm growing weak and old.

SEA WEEDS

IN gardens of a hidden world we dwell,
    In Ocean's crystal depths, through which the
        light
Gleams in pale rays of pearl and chrysolite.
Our purple beauty drapes each rocky cell;
We filmy webs weave for the chambered shell,
    Green carpets spread in coral caverns hid,
    A mossy couch for slumbering Nereid,
Or Siren dreaming some melodious spell.

The sea-nymphs, dancing on the nacreous sands,
    Their flowing locks crown with our airy plumes,
Their foam-white bosoms wreathe with rosy bands
    And garlands woven of our brine-gemmed
        blooms,
And with these treasures of our ocean-birth
Enrich and grace the barren edge of Earth.

The Death of Wagner

THEIR faces veiled in grief, the Muses bend
   Above thy couch of death.   How cold and
       still
  Those lips of fire, that once the world could
      fill
With music, and the light of poësy lend
To misty themes of love and strife, and send
  With power of prophecy a deeper thrill
  To human hearts, and quicken human will
To higher aims of Art and nobler end.

Great Master, mighty Singer, art thou mute?
  Thy harp unstrung? Thy voice forever hushed,
  Whose music like the storm of battle rushed,
Or in soft, melting strains dropped heavenly
      fruit?
  Immortal! still thou compassest Earth's sphere:
  Thy soul on music's wings still hovers here!

THE MERMAID'S SONG

SING, sisters, blow your music shells,
And dance on every wave that swells !
　　While skies are bright,
　　And morn's delight
　　Within our bosom dwells.

Sing, sing and dance, for soon shall we
Return to homes beneath the sea,
　　Where joy is dumb,
　　Our power o'ercome,
　　And hushed our minstrelsy.

There silence reigns in twilight shade
Of coral caverns pearl-inlaid ;
　　Where sweetly sleep,
　　Down in the deep,
　　The captives we have made.

Sing, while we sport in summer rays,
The siren song of olden days,
　　That lures and charms
　　And to our arms
　　The mariner betrays!

A Lover's Rhapsody

Oh, had I the prophetic fire
And touch electric that inspire
The poet-soul's melodious lyre,—

The thoughts that now in secret burn,
Within my heart's deep-hidden urn,
By alchemy of love would turn

Into the golden words that throng
To melt and mingle into song
And fancy's happy dreams prolong.

Yet would I vainly strive to tell
The transports that my bosom swell,
Wrought by thy beauty's potent spell.

And vain were quest, in earth or air,
For aught of wealth that could compare
With worth and loveliness so rare.

In silence chained, when thou art near,
Love seals my lips ; in sudden fear
Awed, as when angel forms appear.

Yet, wouldst thou know what speech denies,
Love's answer all outspoken lies,
And thou mayst read it—in my eyes.

Unloved

LIKE a parched, neglected vine
    Drooping in the sultry air,
Is this thirsting heart of mine,
    Vainly seeking everywhere
Some firm faith on which to lean,
    Some kind hand to raise it higher,
Some fond eye whose steadfast beam
    Glows with love's celestial fire.

Day by day the craving vine
    Puts its pleading tendrils forth,
Mutely grasps the barren air,
    Dragging wearily on earth ;
So this yearning heart of mine
    Hungers with a vain unrest
For some kindred bosom, where
    It might cling forever blest.

BEREAVED

I HEAR the meadow-lark's love-carol ring,
  I note the swallow's sure returning wing,
And blossoms garlanding the new-born spring :—
    But where art Thou ?

The circling years roll on, and evermore
Fresh flowers tessellate earth's fragrant floor ;
The hills grow green, the billows beat the shore
    With pulse unchanged.

Heaven's airy dome, not less serenely blue,
From heights unseen still sheds the golden hue
That lends a glory to earth's daily view,
    As once of yore ;

When like two guileless children hand in hand,
That waken, wonder-lost, in fairyland,
Within a brighter world we seemed to stand—
    Immortal grown.

Beauty, a spirit of inborn delight,
Before us went and led our steps aright,
Through lowly paths to many a starry height
    By angels trod.

As parted dew-drops, trembling side by side,
Drawn by a hidden law, together glide :
Our spirits met and mingled, all untried,
          Insphered by love.

What subtile charm did then our sense entrance,
What fond communings veiled the hours' advance,
What truths, the revelations of a glance,
          Our clear eyes told !

On ocean-sands, in woodland-depths apart,
Or in the crowded halls of Mirth or Art,
With the sweet secret binding heart to heart,
          We stood alone.

E'en in the storm of passion's loving ire,
Flashing its summer-lightning's fitful fire,
Our souls, like burning vapors mounting higher,
          Were purified ;

And clouds that would have made love's sun-
     shine cease
Transfigured shone and gave its light increase,
Or broke in jocund colors arched to peace,—
          Such joy was ours!

But when our life's grand symphony began,
All thought diverse to sweetest concords ran ;
Unfettered as the chords night-breezes fan,
          Its music sprang.

The wing of time no shadow cast ; its power
But mellowed golden tints of that bright hour ;
Eternal summer crown'd our nuptial bower
      With ripened bliss.

And O beloved ! when came the dread decree
That rent the bond of that blest unity,
And like a star no eye again shall see
      Thou didst depart ;

Swift as the fatal wrath of tropic seas,
O'er whose calm breast the hissing tempest flees ;
Dark as the doom the shipwrecked sailor sees :—
      My anguish fell.

I warred with fate, long impiously fought
Against the heavenly barrier thou hadst sought ;
The boon of life was scorned and reckoned
   nought,
      Bereft of Thee !

Till, in that night of struggling grief's appeal,
Subdued and taught an angel's touch to feel,—
Then closed the bleeding wounds that never heal :
      The strife was o'er ;

And the Great Mother took me to her breast,
Soothed me with charms and gave me holy rest :
Now gently leads me to the portals blest
      That shelter Thee.

AT THE FOUNTAIN OF EGERIA

EGERIA, lovely phantom of dead years,
　　Thou lingerest yet in this enchanted grot,
　　Where in ecstatic grief, all else forgot,
Thy being melted wholly into tears,
Whose ceaseless flow no mirrored heaven cheers.
　　Here pilgrims pause to muse on thy sad lot;
　　The poet dreams and consecrates the spot,
And in the murmur of thy fountain hears
Th' immortal plaint, like moan of widowed birds,
　　Its music to his listening ear betrays;
　　And visions throng of old heroic days;
Till thought and feeling blossom into words,
　　To crown thy tears with the unfading wreath
　　That art and song to deathless love bequeath.

In Bondage

AH ME ! it is a weary, bitter thing
    To sit with fettered feet beside the sea
  And mark its blue waves rolling wild and free,
That call and beckon and white arms upfling,
With siren glance a free path offering ;
    To list to winds whose music sweetly tells
    Of Nature's liberty, or proudly swells
With pæans that contending forces ring ;
To trace with longing gaze the free bird's flight
    To summer climes and heavens of purer ray,
    And crave its airy wings to bear away
The ransomed soul ; while day gives place to
        night,
    And, mocked by fortune's smile, the slave of
        fate
    Moves the dull oar of life and learns to watch
        and wait.

Pia in Maremma

"RICORDITI DI ME CHE SON LA PIA"

—Dante, Del Purg. Cant. V

OH, jealous love is cruel in its might !
  More fatal than the south-wind's fiery
    breath,
Through some enchanting garden of delight
  Wooing fair things with kisses steeped in death ;

Till the pale rose falls scentless from its stem,
  Sweet buds of promise cankered strew the
    ground,
And the bowed lily's spotless diadem
  Is blackened in the blight that breathes around.

Thus, like one buried living, make I moan,
  Immured in this lone castle's secrecy ;
While slowly as the closed sepulchral stone
  Maremma's subtile poison stifles me.

The promise of my life's delusive morn
  Was like the sunshine of a false spring day :
A fleeting smile, a golden gleam heaven-born,
  Too soon in chilling storm-clouds hid away.

My dream of bliss, a brief portentous calm,
  Vanished untimely with a troubled waking ;
And grief's embittered tears distill no balm
    To soothe this stricken heart and stay its
      breaking.

The setting sun, blood-red like a fierce eye
  Greedy of pain, seems gloating on my sorrow,
And sinks, as tireless foes to ambush hie,
  Only to bring another suffering morrow.

The dusky sea, with sullen stealthy pace,
  Creeps in for leagues about the marshy land ;
While I dream of blue waves that gaily race
  And break in music on a sunny strand.

Oh, for the pinions of yon wandering bird,
  To soar in freedom from this prison's thrall !
Where, though by day the screech-owl mopes
      unheard
    And bats' black wings cling to the ivied wall,—

By night winds sadly wail, or silence spreads
  A ghostly pall of noisome mists on earth;
Pale spectres glide within, and horrid dreads
  Awake from unseen things of evil birth ;

Where numbed with grief I sit, or stretch wan
      arms,
    Pleading unheard with lips now cold and pale ;

While thoughts, that once came honey-laden
    swarms,
  With torture-stings my very life assail.

Am I that Pia, once in stately halls
  Where met Siena's young patrician daughters,
Whose smile was likened to a light that falls
  Reflecting heaven on untroubled waters?

The breast of Beauty gave her nurture sweet,
  The hand of Art with generous Nature strove
To gift her youth with charms and graces meet,
  And mould her virgin heart a shrine for love.

Ah yes, alas! in life's unclouded spring,
  I was that gladsome, cherished maid, so graced,
Until a fatal love with spousal ring
  A jeweled fetter on this finger placed.

These faded locks, once bright and softly flowing,
  Were beauty's pride, breeze-kissed and rosy-
    crowned ;
These languid feet, once light as zephyr's going,
  Air-winged by mirth and music spurned the
    ground.

Till love came fluttering to my ready heart,
  As comes the shy bird to its hidden nest,—
Only ere long as coldly to depart
  And leave to wintry winds what summer blest.

I learned to brook suspicion's gloomy form,
  The withering frowns that banished artless joy;
Unconscious of th' impending passion-storm,
  With bolt of jealous scorn that would destroy.

O cruel doubt that crushed a true heart's love !
  Quenched kindling hopes in vain indignant
      tears,
And left me nought a husband's faith to prove
  But sullied fame and life's few ruined years.

Night folds me shuddering in her black embrace,
  Not darker than my fortune's present gloom ;
For secret death lurks in this shadowy place
  And hurries on my early, unknown doom.

To a Thistledown

WELCOME, tiny wandering thing !
   With thy silken-feathered wing,
In my chamber window stealing,
Noiselessly thy form revealing,
Gently waking in my heart
Thoughts that not with thee depart,
   But deepen memory into feeling.

Thoughts of childhood's happy dream,
When a changeless fairy scene
   Life appeared, without a morrow
   That could wear a shade of sorrow.
Light and free as thou, more dear,
Dwelt I in love's atmosphere,
   Untaught a joy from hope to borrow.

Wafted through the golden air,
Whither dost thou softly bear
   Thy little fructifying treasure,
   To complete the careful measure
Of thy humble task on earth ?
Hast thou not the meed of worth
   In a wanton tour of pleasure ?

Restless, sportive, airy thing,
Tarry and thy story sing !

On the bank of some blue river,
Where the pointed aspens quiver,
Hast thou left thy parent stem
For the crowded homes of men,
There thy moral to deliver?

Or from some secluded lake,
Whose glassy depths weird pictures make
Of hoary rock or drooping willow,
That dimly shades the mossy pillow,
Where the wild-fowl's hidden nest
Hides her brood from preying quest,
Com'st thou dancing o'er the billow?

Or perchance where some rude hedge
Marks the meadow's grassy edge,
Or field with rustling corn resounding,
The farmer's fruitful home surrounding,—
A spiny calyx of pale hue
Beside the blushing wild-rose grew,
Whence thou, oft kissing earth, com'st
bounding.

Link of that mysterious chain,
Whose secret man hath sought in vain,
Which though strained is sundered never,
Spite of time or death's endeavor,—
Lo, thy little downy sphere
Less marvelous doth not appear
Than sparkling orbs that roll forever!

Matin Song

THE glad earth wakes! O welcome day,
  That brings fresh life in every token!
Night-shadows flee like captive sprites
  Whose fairy bonds the morn hath broken.

Resistless beams of rosy light
  The gloomy bars of darkness shatter;
And fleecy cloudlets upward float,
  Like sportive flocks that part and scatter.

A thousand gems on leaf and blade
  Like merry twinkling stars are glancing;
The streams run blue, the babbling brooks
  Upon their pebbly beds are dancing.

Birds plume and stretch their ruffled throats,
  With sudden strains of music gushing;
Flowers raise their slumb'rous heads and smile,
  Like waking babes with pleasure flushing.

The fallow fields and grassy meads
  Long level rays with gold are glossing;
The breeze with dewy fragrance fraught
  The tassel'd corn is gently tossing:

From wood and plain a hymn of praise
  To Nature's God is sweetly sounding ;
And every freshened pulse of life
  With gratitude and joy is bounding.

A Bird Carol

Where the topmost branches swing,
There I lightly sit and sing
Greetings to returning spring :
      Tìra-la-la !

Darting now from spray to spray,
Where the dancing sunbeams play,
Warbling a gay roundelay :
      Tìra-la-la !

Groves and gardens I explore ;
Near the friendly cottage door
Linger, singing o'er and o'er
      Tìra-la-la !

Or within some leafy bower,
Sheltered from a passing shower,
Sipping nectar from a flower :
      Tìra-la-la !

Through deep woodland shades I go,
Where unruffled waters flow,
Waking echoes sweet and low :
      Tìra-la-la !

When I woo my little wife,
Heart and song with joy are rife:
Oh, what happiness is life !
      Tìra-la-la !

Arching boughs that touch the sky,
Haunts unseen by human eye,
There my little treasures lie :
      Tìra-la-la !

Safe within a downy nest,
Warm upon the mother-breast,
While I sing with love's unrest—
      Tìra-la-la !

CRADLE SONG

SLUMBER, my darling one !
    Slumber and rest,
In tenderest faith
    On thy fond mother's breast ;
For soft is the pillow,
    Where fresh from the heart
Her life and thy own
    Mingle never to part.
             Lullaby ! Lullaby !

The weary sun sinks,
    His bright journey is o'er ;
The wavelets he kissed
    Ripple golden no more.
Then lullaby, babe !
    Sleep the dark hours away,
To wake and rejoice
    With the beautiful day.
             Lullaby ! Lullaby!

Night's shadows are falling,
    And chill blows the breeze
That murmurs so mournfully
    Through the old trees ;

But warm and secure
    From disturbing alarms,
My little dove nestles
    In sheltering arms.
            Lullaby! Lullaby!

ARCTURUS

TO MY GRANDSON AT COLLEGE WHOSE BOYISH
NOM DE PLUME HAD BEEN ARCTURUS

AS nightly, like some Magian worshipper,
  I gaze enraptured on the starry sky
And mark Arcturus gleam with ardent eye,
Fond thoughts of thee my yearning bosom stir,
Till tearful dews the heavenly vision blur.
  I see thee, clothed in youth's auroral light,
  Awaiting manhood's day with vision bright,
To pure and lofty paths of thought defer.

Now far away in other heavens unseen
  By my fond glance, my young Arcturus dwells,
  Shedding on stranger hearts those gladsome
      spells
Wherein my weary spirit sought to glean
  New strength and courage for declining years,
  Amid affection's glow, undimmed by tears.

To My Brother

T. J. G.

LAST night in dreamland, by thy cheering side,
  I wandered 'mid long unremembered scenes.
By alchemy of slumber's charmèd means,
Youth crowned our brows ; joy pulsed in life's
      full tide ;
The forms beloved, that time and death divide,
  Grew bright, emerged from memory's misty
      screens ;
  And yet, it seemed, the harvest wisdom gleans
From scattered sorrows did with us abide.

Sweet the renewal of that early life !
  When for the mastery in logic's wit
  The intellectual fires of youth were lit,
And mirth and humor closed the gay tongue-strife.
  Some compensation absence yet may deem
  The fleeting pageant of a happy dream.

CURDS AND CREAM

A SOUVENIR OF PHILADELPHIA DEDICATED TO
MY BROTHERS AND SISTERS

I

NOTHING trivial, mean, or rude,
    But contains some hidden good :
In the husk the fruitful seed ;
Potent virtue in the weed ;
In the rock the virgin gold ;
Bitter rinds sweet juices hold ;
In the rough unsightly shell
Pearly hues of heaven dwell ;
And the wasting sands of earth
Cover gems of priceless worth.
All things are not what they seem,—
Here is more than Curds and Cream !

II

Soft and cool and mild and sweet,
With Arcadian gleams replete ;
Rosy dawns and purple shades
Garnered here by rustic maids ;
Clover-tops and new-mown hay
Tempered by the breath of May ;

Vesper music of the trees
Trembling to the evening breeze ;
Homely sound of lowing kine
Mingling with the strain divine, —
Humble poet's worthy theme,
Let me laud thee, Curds and Cream !

III

Let me ever thankful be
Simple tastes have cherished thee ;
For the charm thy sweetness brings
Touches memory's secret springs.
Bathed in fancy's magic dews,
Youth's pale flower its bloom renews.
Visions throng of old delights, —
Rural sounds and rural sights,
Where an ancient farm-house stood,
Near an oft-frequented wood :
Lights and shadows of the dream
Conjured here by Curds and Cream !

IV

Sounds that taught my untuned ear
Music of a higher sphere ;
When I shared the pure repose
Nature's sober gladness knows ;
And the song of some lone bird
Unknown deeps of feeling stirred,
Like a warning voice afar
Calling from my unseen star ;

Long ere love's impassioned strain
Woke the echoing voice of pain,
Or doubt's rude tones to discord brought
Heavenly harmonies of thought,
Or grief could any blight impart
To mar the summer of my heart.

Sights that painted on mine eye
Beauty-types that never die :—
Shady stream with cedar dyed,
And fringe of emerald moss beside :
Airy grace of tangled vines ;
Cloistral glooms among the pines ;
Pictured vistas through arcades,
Set like gems in forest shades ;
Sycamores in silvery mail,
Giant wardens of the vale ;
Weeping willows drooping low
In green cascades of leafy flow ;
Glistening fields of growing grain ;
Flocks like snow-flakes on the plain ;
Distant orchard's cloudy bloom ;
Country garden—all perfume !
Where 'mid healing herbs the rose
In redundant beauty grows ;
And silken lilies rear their heads
Proudly from the rustic beds ;
Lilac-hedge and grassy floor
Leading to the dairy door ;
Golden cheeses, splashing churn,
Frothy milk-pail's rich return ;

Fallow fields and ploughing team ;
Morning banquet—Curds and Cream !

v

What this witchery ? And whence
Come these subtile links of sense,
Blending earthly with divine,
Bridging o'er the gulf of time,
And bringing sunny pictures back
To illume its blighted track ?
Links of sense with feeling fraught,
Forged and fashioned into thought,
Whose electric thrills unroll
Secret records of the soul,
With ironic grace supreme
In a bowl of Curds and Cream !

VI

Fled the long, long years of strife
On the battle-field of life ;
Vanished all their wounds and pain,
Every tint of sorrow's stain :—
Childhood's golden age is here,
With its joys and simple cheer ;
Destined fortune strange and bright ;
Youth's horizon—boundless light !

Early morn ! Hour fresh and cool,
Sacred from the thrall of school !
'Mid the bloom of flowers and fruits,

Odors wild of plants and roots,
At the market-place we stand,—
Brothers, sisters, hand in hand.
Brass-bound tub and napkin white
Bring the snowy curds to sight;
Cheerful, sun-browned dames dispense
For our smiles and copper pence:
Rosy cheeks and lips redeem
Gross delight in Curds and Cream!

VII

Lilies floating on the tide,
Innocence our shield and guide,
'Mid the throng of busy feet
Crowding market-house and street,
Noise of traffic and demand,
Loiter we in fairy-land.
Undiscerned the brow of care,
Eager search for scanty fare,
Hungry glance and pallid cheek
That privation's doom bespeak :—
Heedless of the living stream,
Sip we nectar,—Curds and Cream!

VIII

Golden days forever fled,
When our footsteps angels led!
Childish faith and fresh surprise
That made the green earth Paradise!
Where is now that household band?

Mother's soft caressing hand?
Careful Father, teacher sage,
Planting seeds for later age,—
Seeds of love and truth and thought,
That enriching harvests brought?
Where the kindred of our hearth?
And playmates dear who shared our mirth?

Closed the shining Gates of Old!
Time and Death their gains have told.
Pearly morn and ardent noon
Darken to night's coming gloom.
Now no longer hand in hand
Brothers dear and sisters stand :
Ripened like the autumn sheaves,
Scattered like the wintry leaves,
Oceans vast between us roll,
Other ties our lives control.
Yet, as in a magic glass,
All our youthful joys repass,
Luminous in memory's beam
By the spell of Curds and Cream!

CALIFORNIA

HAIL, Daughter of the Great Republic,
       crowned
   With vine and olive, while thy sunny face
   Blends matron dignity with youthful grace,
And Nature's bounty makes thee world-renowned!

An empire's strength within thy realm is found:
   Health, riches, beauty,—all in thy embrace;
   And from thy toiling sons has sprung a race
Whose worth to thy wide glory shall redound.

And when disunion threatened to destroy
   The noblest fabric ever reared by man,
       How firmly on its platform didst thou stand!
How lavishly thy treasure didst employ,
   To soothe the woes that Civil War began,
       And by thy brave example cheer the land!

In the Santa Cruz Mountains

HERE in the balmy air I breathe fresh life,
New sense of liberty and Nature's grace ;
And like some lonely Dryad, in deep shades
Apart from man, I wander in a world
Of sylvan beauty.

          In this silent world,
Lo ! the sequoia's venerable bulk
Stands yet firm-rooted 'gainst the stroke of time,
Whilst nations and proud thrones, their courses
       run,
Have crumbled into dusty nothingness.
Great pines, whose plumy helms salute the sky,
Their naked boles like granite shafts upreared,
Stand monarchs of the mountain solitude ;
And ancient oaks, with tangled, hoary locks
Of pallid moss, rise like the effigies
Of Druid priests of a forgotten age ;
And groves of cypress spread a feathery screen,
Where nestle quail or sits the listening hare.

With trunk and twisted stems of rosy hue,
The stout madroño spreads umbrageous leaves,
That glisten fitfully with emerald sheen,
Half-veiling flowery urns, like pearl-drops hung,
That load the sighing breeze with drowsy sweets.

The ceanothus, too, with subtile breath,
Wafts fragrance from her tiny purple plumes;
And delicate azaleas, with faint fire,
Like silver stars, light up each bosky nook ;
And manzanitas raise entwining arms,
Dyed in the ruddy hue of native wine;
While mountain pinks, scattered like crimson
      drops
Fresh from earth's heart, glow on her naked
      breast.

In this embowered glen, beside this stream
That glides in crystal to the neighboring sea,
Oh, let me rest, and in an idle dream
Of old-world story, playful fancies feed !—
That now resounding in the wild bee's hum
I hear the magic horn of Oberon ;
That on this green bank, ''sometime of the
      night,''
The fairy queen Titania may have lain ;
In yon cool alcove, where each furtive beam
Dapples the gloom with flickering golden light,
Her dainty elfin troops of antic sprites
Like glow-worms may have sparkled for awhile.

Or lost in sterner mood, here let me muse
On life's mutations in the lapse of time,
Pacing with tardy steps these dusky aisles,
Whose brown elastic carpet of dead leaves
Is but a page of Earth's wide palimpsest,
Where, o'er the dim mementoes of lost years,

The olden tale, forevermore renewed,
In fresh designs of beauty she records.

Or like some spirit-weary potentate,
Sated with pomp and the behests of power,
Withdrawn from vain illusions of the world
To seek the balm of Nature's holy chrism,—
My royal throne this rugged, time-worn stone,
Fern-plumed and draped with pall of velvet
        moss,—
Let me, communing with sweet Nature's self,
Seek inspiration from her purest founts ;
And here supine, with raptured eye explore
The blue ethereal vault above me spread,
Until my spirit, borne to the abyss
Of thought divine from which its being sprang,
Touched momentarily with kindred fire,
Thrills with mysterious recognition of
The Unseen Presence that pervades all space :
And reconciled to Nature's laws, discerns
That all is good, blest by Eternal Love.

In Pace

COME, Sleep, O silent goddess, grave and calm!
  Shed o'er my troubled brow thy soothing
    balm,
Haunt my vexed ear with some quaint holy
    psalm,
        Or olden lay
        Of childhood's day.

Beneath thy nebulous, soft veil conceal
Earth's sordid cares, the woes time cannot heal ;
On weary lids lay thy Lethean seal,
        Like the caress
        Fond mothers press.

Lead me through mazes of thy charmèd land
To far-off shores by peaceful heavens spanned,
There let me wander or enraptured stand,
        Forgetting all
        Life's fret and thrall.

There welcome smiling eyes and lips long stilled,
Whose tender greetings once my bosom thrilled ;
There let me find youth's promises fulfilled,
        Nor more bewail
        The hopes that fail.

Or in oblivion steeped, let memory cease ;
And like a nestling veiled in downy fleece,
In all the sweet beatitude of peace,
   Thy spell's control
   Wrap my sad soul.